EZRA'S DUEL
WITH **DANGER**

BASED ON THE *STAR WARS REBELS* EPISODES
"EMPIRE DAY" BY HENRY GILROY,
"GATHERING FORCES" BY GREG WEISMAN, AND
"PATH OF THE JEDI" BY CHARLES MURRAY

WRITTEN BY MICHAEL KOGGE

EGMONT

EGMONT

We bring stories to life

First published in Great Britain 2015
by Egmont UK Limited, The Yellow Building,
1 Nicholas Road, London W11 4AN.

© & ™ 2015 Lucasfilm Ltd.   .
ISBN 978 1 4052 7631 3
59571/1
Printed in Italy

Stay safe online. Any website addresses listed in this book are correct at the
time of going to print. However, Egmont is not responsible for content hosted by
third parties. Please be aware that online content can be subject to change and
websites can contain content that is unsuitable for children. We advise that all
children are supervised when using the internet.

To find more great *Star Wars* books, visit www.egmont.co.uk/starwars

CONTENTS

PART 1: EMPIRE DAY   1

CHAPTER **1**   2

CHAPTER **2**   16

CHAPTER **3**   22

CHAPTER **4**   32

CHAPTER **5**   42

CHAPTER **6**   52

CHAPTER **7**   62

CHAPTER **8**   74

PART 2: ENLIGHTENMENT   83

CHAPTER **9**   84

CHAPTER **10**   94

CHAPTER **11**   102

CHAPTER **12**   112

PART 1
EMPIRE DAY

CHAPTER 1

'**Step outside** of yourself,' Kanan
Jarrus said. 'Make a connection with another
being.'

Ezra stood with Kanan in a field outside
Old Jho's Pit Stop, a remote repair facility
where his friends had landed their star
freighter, the *Ghost*. A few mechanics wandered
around the yard, but Ezra's friends hadn't gone
there for maintenance on their ship. The pit
stop's main attraction was a cantina where
Old Jho served drinks. Nowhere else on Lothal
could you enjoy refreshments while your
vehicle's power converters were being changed.

Hera, the *Ghost*'s Twi'lek pilot, had gone

inside the cantina with Zeb, the burly Lasat who was Ezra's friendly nemesis, and Sabine, the gutsy artist who was the most colourful member of the crew. Ezra wished he could've joined them. He longed for an ice-cold fizzy that he could sip in a dark corner away from everyone else. Today was a day he'd just as soon fast-forward and forget.

'Can we do this another day?' Ezra asked.

'We can do it now.' Kanan held a rock in his hand. 'Focus.'

Ezra huffed. The sooner this stupid training session was over, the sooner he could get away from everyone. 'Just throw the rock, will you?'

Kanan tossed the rock into a patch of weeds. A wild Loth-cat jumped out, snarling and hissing, in defence of his territory.

'I don't think he wants to connect,' Ezra said.

'You're resisting. He can sense it,' Kanan said.

'He can *sense* it? What is he, like a Padawan cat?'

As if it understood, the Loth-cat pounced at Ezra. It was a ferocious little feline, all tooth and claw. Ezra tussled with the beast, trying to avoid being bitten or scratched.

'You don't seem to be getting this,' Kanan said.

'I get that this furball is trying to kill me!'
With great effort, Ezra shoved the Loth-cat off
him into the dirt. 'Now give me your lightsaber
and I'll make the connection you want.'

Kanan gave Ezra a stare that would make a
Hutt feel guilty. 'Excuse me?'

Ezra swallowed. One thing he'd learned
was that sarcasm wasn't part of the Jedi Code.
'I just don't see the point of this.'

'The point is that you're not alone. You're
connected to every living thing in the universe.
But to discover that, you have to let your
guard down. You have to be willing to attach
to others.' Kanan waved a finger and smiled
at the Loth-cat. Within seconds the beast was
purring at his feet. Kanan made it appear so
easy.

Ezra looked away, resigned. 'Then maybe
I'll never be a Jedi.'

Kanan turned to Ezra. 'Kid, whatever's
going on with you, you need to spill it.'

Spill it. That was Kanan and Hera's jargon for revealing what troubled them, so that another person could offer support. But Ezra's problem couldn't be solved by talking because there *wasn't* a solution to Ezra's problem.

'I'm sorry, Kanan. I don't mean to wear you out. Today's just not a good day,' Ezra said.

'Today?'

Ezra grunted. 'Empire Day.'

As if on cue, a squadron of Imperial TIE fighters shrieked through the sky. Three of the hexagonal-winged starfighters broke from formation to land at the pit stop. The black-suited pilots climbed out from the TIEs' eyeball-shaped cockpits.

'What are so many TIEs doing out this far?' Ezra asked.

'Nothing good. Come on,' Kanan said.

They followed the three TIE pilots into the crowded cantina. Humans, humanoids, and even droids packed the booths. Unlike some people, Old Jho didn't discriminate. As long as one had credits to spare, he'd serve whatever a customer wanted, whether it was bantha milk or lubricator fluid.

Kanan led Ezra to the counter. The *Ghost*'s crew members were regulars there and Old Jho immediately filled two cups. Glancing around, Ezra saw that Hera and Zeb occupied a booth behind a pebble-skinned Rodian who was slurping spicebrew. Sabine stood beside them, wearing her Mandalorian armour, though she'd left her helmet behind on the *Ghost*.

The Imperials didn't head to the bar. They scanned the crowd, and the pilot who appeared to be the leader waved his two comrades towards the Rodian's table. The two wrenched the Rodian to his feet while their leader activated a datapad. A mug shot of a Rodian appeared on the screen.

Ezra blinked, recognising the Rodian on the datapad. 'Tseebo.'

'What?' Kanan asked.

'Nothing,' Ezra said. He had done all he could to bury that part of his past. He was not going to start digging it up now.

The lead pilot compared the datapad's mug shot with the face of the captive Rodian. 'He's not the one,' the pilot said, grunting with disappointment. He pocketed the datapad while the other pilots shoved the Rodian back in his seat. Then the three Imperials went to the bar, where the lead pilot banged his fist. 'The Imperial Holonet should play here at all times. It's the law.'

Old Jho flipped a switch, powering a holoprojector over the bar. It displayed the insignia of the Empire, before cutting to the well-groomed Alton Kastle, anchor for Imperial Holonews.

'Today is Empire Day,' Kastle said, 'celebrating the fifteenth anniversary of the galaxy's salvation, when our great Emperor

Palpatine ended the Clone Wars and founded our glorious Empire.'

The lead pilot lifted his drink and turned to the other patrons. 'You heard the man! Raise your cups to the Emperor!'

Few joined the pilot's toast as the news broadcast began to ripple with static. 'On Lothal, Governor Pryce has commissioned a parade –'

Ezra smirked when Kastle's image was replaced by that of an older, moustached man, who had made it his duty to interrupt these broadcasts. 'Citizens, this is Senator-in-Exile Gall Trayvis. I bring more news the Empire doesn't want you to hear. I urge you to boycott all Empire Day celebrations to protest the ongoing injustices of the Imperial regime.'

The lead pilot banged his fist again. 'Shut this off!'

'Can't,' Old Jho said. 'It's the law.'

Aggravated, the lead pilot turned to his comrades. 'We're done here.'

Ezra watched the Imperial pilots exit the cantina in disgust. A collective sigh of relief followed and all patrons returned to their refreshments. Old Jho switched off the holoprojector.

Hera, Zeb and Sabine rose from the table to join Ezra and Kanan at the bar. 'TIE pilots on search patrols? What's going on?' Kanan asked Old Jho.

'Imperials have locked down the ports and put Destroyers in orbit. It's a full planetary blockade.'

Kanan glanced back at the spiny-headed customer who had been accosted. 'They're after a Rodian.'

'Just be glad they're not after us for once,' Sabine remarked.

'With what we've got planned for today's parade, they'll be after us again tomorrow,' Kanan said.

'Well, you're going to have to do it without me.' Ezra headed towards the exit.

'Where do you think you're going?' Kanan asked.

'I just need some time alone. Today's brought back some memories,' Ezra said.

Thankfully, they left him alone as he hiked across the plains to the abandoned communications tower he called home. Once inside, he pulled out a dusty crate. He searched through the contents and retrieved a simple keycard.

On Empire Day, he had a tradition of using this keycard to visit another place he had once called home. He had thought this year he was done with the tradition, that his new family had replaced his old one for good. As he looked at the keycard, he knew that wasn't the case. His vision blurred from tears welling in his eyes. He did not wipe them away.

'*Ezra,*' a woman, whose voice he hadn't heard in a long, long time, said.

'Mum?' He spun, looking around. The tower's repair garage was empty. He was alone.

'*Ezra.*' Now it was a man's voice, one he knew simply as –

'Dad?' He looked, but as before, there was no one. Was his mind playing tricks on him? Was he hearing ghosts?

'*Ezra, we have to stand up for people in need,*' his father continued, '*especially those in trouble with the Empire.*'

This wasn't a trick, it was just a memory. His father had probably spoken those words when Ezra was younger, and now his conscience was reminding him.

Tseebo. The Rodian was in trouble and needed his help.

CHAPTER 2

Parades were one thing the Empire did well, Kanan had to admit. From the corner of an alley, he and Hera watched an impressive display of stormtroopers, cadets and vehicles march down the main boulevard of Capital City towards the Imperial complex. Fortunately, the grand spectacle didn't persuade the local citizens to forget the evils of the Empire. The small crowds who had come out for the event had to be prodded by Taskmaster Grint to cheer.

On a stage before the complex, Minister Maketh Tua addressed those in attendance. 'Lothal is just as important to our Empire as any world in the galaxy. And Governor Pryce wanted me to show you why.'

Behind her, the complex's hangar doors opened. A repulsorlift platform floated forward, carrying a modified TIE fighter, which had smaller, curved wings instead of the usual flat design.

'Citizens, I present you with the latest vessel from Lothal's Imperial shipyards. Sienar Fleet Systems' advanced TIE starfighter!'

Kanan joined the crowds in giving polite applause. 'Pretty, isn't it?'

'Yeah,' Hera said. 'Almost feel bad about blowing it up.'

They split, with Hera going to prep the *Ghost* and pick them up at the rendezvous point. Kanan went in the other direction, snaking through the crowds towards the complex. Suddenly loud, colourful fireworks lit up the sky, a clever distraction provided by Sabine and Zeb. Kanan slipped beneath

TIE FIGHTER SQUADRON

the repulsorlift platform that held the TIE.
He quickly planted another one of Sabine's
customised thermal detonators on the
platform's underside.

Unfortunately, the fireworks hadn't
distracted everyone. 'You there!' shouted

a stormtrooper commander. 'This area's off-limits!'

Kanan pretended to be awed by the firework blasts. 'Beautiful, isn't it? All the colours. It's like a rainbow.'

This stormtrooper wouldn't be fooled. He reached for his gun, until a human boy slid next to Kanan. 'Dad, what are you doing?' Ezra asked, then turned to the stormtrooper. 'Sorry, mister, my dad's just so patriotic, you know.'

'Empire Day! I love it! All hail our glorious Empire!' Kanan lied, faking a smile.

The stormtrooper commander looked at both of them, though it was impossible to read his face under his helmet. At last, he gestured. 'All right, well, move along!'

Kanan and Ezra didn't have to be told twice. They waded back into the crowd. 'Thanks,' Kanan said. 'Where've you been?'

'Making connections,' Ezra said, as if he'd been following Kanan's lesson all along. 'How's the plan going?'

This time Kanan's smile wasn't fake. 'Just watch.'

The repulsorlift platform behind them suddenly exploded, accompanied by flashes of colour and streaming ribbons of sparks, flipping over the advanced TIE. The craft crashed into the stage and sent Minister Tua and other Imperial leaders flying into the air.

Chaos seized the Imperial ranks. Officers started barking conflicting orders. Stormtroopers rushed about in confusion. But most satisfying for Kanan was spotting the ghoulish figure in the dark flight suit who emerged from the smouldering TIE.

The Inquisitor fumed in rage over the wreckage of his starfighter.

Imperials might put on a good parade, Kanan mused as Sabine and Zeb rejoined them, *but the rebels put on a better show.*

CHAPTER **3**

The chaos didn't last long. The Imperials ordered a citywide lockdown. Air traffic was prohibited, preventing Hera from bringing the *Ghost* to the rendezvous point. With more and more stormtroopers pouring into the streets by the minute, the rebels would be caught soon if they didn't find a good place to hide.

Ezra knew of a place. It wouldn't fit broad-shouldered Zeb, but the Lasat said he could hide in the Old Market, where he would blend in around the other nonhumans.

'We'll signal a new rendezvous when we can,' Kanan said. The brawny Lasat slung his bo-rifle over his back and climbed over the alley wall.

'Follow me,' Ezra said to Kanan and Sabine. He yanked open a sewer grate and dropped down, leading them through a hidden ventilation shaft. It felt like old times again, when he used to make quick getaways after stealing mealpacks from Supply Master Lyste's trucks.

He had them climb out in front of a habitation unit. A red Imperial insignia fastened to its door declared the place off-limits.

Ezra surprised Kanan by inserting a keycard into the door lock. It clicked open.

'You were coming here today,' Kanan said, giving Ezra a knowing look. 'This was your home, wasn't it? Where you grew up.'

'I grew up on the streets,' Ezra said, correcting him. 'Alone.' Ezra pushed the door open and entered.

Dim light shone in from the street through the cracks in the boarded-up windows. The place was practically empty, as thieves had plundered anything of value years ago.

'Then why are we here?' Sabine asked, taking off her helmet. 'Why now?'

'I had a feeling,' Ezra said, letting his words linger. He crossed the room and pulled up a trapdoor in the floor. 'Tseebo?' he called down. 'It's me, Ezra Bridger.'

After a moment, a green-skinned Rodian clambered out, muttering in Huttese. The back of his spiny head was stitched with circuitry.

'That's the Rodian the Imperials are hunting,' Kanan said. 'You know him?'

'Name's Tseebo. A friend of my parents.' Ezra watched Tseebo bumble about with no sense of direction. 'But something's wrong. What's that thing on his head?'

Sabine held Tseebo in place so she could examine the tech. 'The Empire's been known to implant lower-level technicians with cybernetic circuits. Personality sacrificed for productivity.'

'Tseebo's productivity is ninety percent higher than average Imperial data worker,' Tseebo blurted out robotically.

'Tseebo went to work for the Imperial

information office after the Empire took my parents away,' Ezra said.

'Your parents?' Kanan asked, surprised. 'You never told us.'

'What's to tell? They've been gone for eight years.' Ezra flicked a finger at Tseebo's headgear. The Rodian didn't react at all from his touch. 'I've been on my own since I was seven.'

Tseebo started speaking again in Huttese. Kanan turned to Sabine. 'What's he saying?' She was the only one who understood the Hutt language, thanks to her Mandalorian education.

Sabine listened, her eyes widening. 'He's detailing Imperial fighter deployments on Lothal!'

Kanan grew excited. 'Can you access it?'

While Kanan helped Sabine hack into Tseebo's headgear, Ezra climbed down through the trapdoor. Tseebo cocked his head in Ezra's direction, as if just realising who he was.

'Ezra Bridger. Son of Ephraim and Mira Bridger. Born fifteen years ago today,' Tseebo stated.

Ezra ignored him and dropped off the ladder into the secret room. But he could still hear Sabine's muffled voice. 'Empire Day ... it's Ezra's birthday,' she said.

Ezra winced. So now they knew his little secret. His curse. Of all the days to be born, his was the day the Empire came into being – 'a Galactic Empire to last ten thousand years,' its Emperor had declared. And as Ezra had grown, so had the Empire, conquering system after system over the last fourteen years, taking everything he loved in the process.

He'd never be able to change his birth date, but one day he'd like to celebrate it without being reminded it was also 'Empire Day.'

He turned on the lights. The small room was bare except for an antiquated holonet console. When he powered it on, the console made a grinding sound and ejected a disk. He took the disk – and voices suddenly echoed in his mind.

'*Big risk you Bridgers take,*' said a Rodian voice. '*Tseebo say you must think of your son.*'

'*He's all we think about,*' said Ezra's father. '*We're teaching Ezra to stand up for people in need.*'

'*We're fighting for our son's freedom,*' said his mother.

'*Tseebo not fight battle Tseebo know cannot be won. Neither should Bridgers.*'

Ezra considered the holodisk as the voices faded. Could this conversation have actually happened between his parents and Tseebo – or was he making it up? Maybe he'd overheard it as a child and only understood it now. It was why he didn't like coming home. Too many sad memories.

A noise behind him made him turn. Sabine stood near the ladder. 'What's with the old disk?'

Ezra dropped the disk on the console. 'My

folks used to do underground broadcasts from here, speaking out against the Empire. It's probably just one of their recordings.'

He walked past her and climbed up the ladder. Sabine followed, transmitting a code from her gauntlet to activate the holo-emitter on Tseebo's headgear.

What the holo-emitter projected astounded Ezra. Schematics of weapons and vehicles flashed by, including the specs for the new TIEs and T-8 disruptors. Also displayed were schedules of troop movements, encrypted memos and the Empire's five-year plans for Outer Rim planets like Lothal.

'No wonder his brain's shorting out,' Ezra said. 'All that data would overload anyone.'

'The secrets in his head could bring down the Empire,' Kanan said.

Tseebo wobbled and Ezra gave him a steady hand. If they could smuggle Tseebo safely off Lothal with his secrets, today might not be a bad day after all.

CHAPTER 4

Kanan watched a squad of stormtroopers leap out of a troop transport that stopped near Ezra's home. Their commander was so adamant that all resources were used to find the renegade Rodian, he left only two soldiers to guard the transport.

Kanan shot one of the troopers with his blaster while Sabine bruised her knuckles punching out the other one. 'I miss Zeb,' she said.

After Kanan tossed out the pilot, Sabine took his seat. Ezra and Tseebo sat in the cab while Kanan operated the transport's weaponry. They sped through the streets, encountering no resistance until they approached the city gates. There, Commandant Aresko and Taskmaster Grint had assembled a host of stormtroopers, armed transports and walkers to block the exits.

Aresko stepped forward. 'That's far enough, rebel scum! Stop now I say!'

'I have *no* plans on stopping,' Sabine told Kanan. She accelerated and ploughed through the enemy line. Taken by surprise, the Imperial gunners missed wildly. The few blasts that did hit the transport were easily absorbed by the vehicle's thick armour.

The stolen transport fled towards the highway exiting the city to the south. Stormtroopers dived out of the way of the speeding vehicle. The transport crashed through the leg of an AT-DP, causing it to topple across the highway, blocking the Imperial forces that were behind it.

Imperial bikers closed in on the stolen

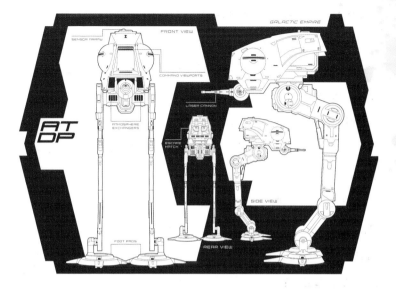

transport, flanking a second transport that
opened fire. More urgently, an armed transport
had taken up the rear, posing itself as a
difficult target for Kanan. Whoever controlled
that transport knew what he was doing.

A biker accelerated alongside the stolen
transport and blew open the cab door with
a detonator. He jumped inside, reaching for
Tseebo and shouting, 'The Rodian!'

Kanan hurtled over his seat into the biker. The two wrestled, and for a moment, it seemed that the trooper was more than Kanan could handle. He knocked Kanan backward, towards the open door.

Kanan, however, was strong in ways the biker would never be. He channelled the momentum of his fall into the Force, reflecting the energy back at the trooper. The Imperial flew out of the transport, into his fellow biker, and both smacked the ground below.

The transport suddenly shook, rear-ended by the pursuing transport. Kanan glanced back to see the one person he'd feared was commanding it: Agent Kallus of the Imperial Security Bureau, wielding the bo-rifle he'd taken during the massacres on Zeb's homeworld.

Kallus leapt out of the pursuing transport's cab and onto their roof. There was no way Kanan could climb up there before the agent did something drastic.

But Kallus wouldn't have that chance. The *Ghost* swooped down from the clouds, Zeb leaning out of its bottom hatch. 'Remember me?' the Lasat shouted, firing his bo-rifle at Kallus, while the *Ghost's* rear guns also opened up.

The barrage of laserfire did what Kanan had been unable to do – hit the pursuing transport, front and centre, and knock it out of commission. The vehicle skidded out of control on the highway, digging a deep trench before stopping altogether. Since Hera was piloting the *Ghost*, Kanan guessed Chopper was on the rear guns, probably beeping congratulations to himself.

Zeb's shots, meanwhile, struck near Kallus's feet, causing the agent to lose his balance. He tumbled off the back of the stolen transport, out of sight – hopefully for good.

'OK, you're all clear,' Zeb said. 'Pull over and we'll –'

Hera's voice crackled over the transport's

comm. 'Belay that. Have to be a scoop job. Sensors reading multiple TIEs incoming.'

She brought the *Ghost* as close to the transport as she could. Kanan climbed onto the transport's roof and helped pull Tseebo and Ezra up after him. Sabine switched the transport to autopilot, then joined them.

Over the horizon streaked five TIE fighters, one an advanced model that Kanan sensed was piloted by the Inquisitor.

Zeb reached out from the hatch of the *Ghost*. 'Get in!' He grabbed Tseebo and yanked him inside, then hoisted up Ezra and Sabine next.

A round of blaster fire prevented Kanan from following. He spun, instinctively detaching two parts of his lightsaber hilt from his belt and connecting them.

Kallus had not fallen completely off the transport. The ISB agent gripped the transport's edge, firing his bo-rifle at Kanan with his free hand.

His shots would have taken out anyone – anyone but a Jedi. Kanan deflected the blaster bolts with his blade back at Kallus, then leapt up through the *Ghost*'s hatch.

Kanan didn't check to see if Kallus had been hit. He knew it would take more than a few blaster bolts to silence that particular Imperial agent. And there were more pressing concerns.

Kanan raced right to the lower turret. The TIEs were closing in.

CHAPTER **5**

Enemy fire pummelled the *Ghost*'s shields. The freighter shook so much that Ezra needed both Sabine and Zeb to get Tseebo seated in the common room. Suddenly, they heard Chopper cry out as a console near the back of the ship exploded.

Zeb ran to check on the damaged droid. Sabine removed her helmet and began to follow. 'I have to man the nose guns.'

'I'm coming with,' Ezra said.

Tseebo grabbed his arm and stopped him. 'Ezra – *Ezra Bridger*. It is you!'

Ezra tried to wrest himself free. 'Now's not the best time for a reunion.'

The Rodian pulled him closer and babbled more Huttese. Ezra couldn't understand a word, but Sabine halted in the doorway, looking stunned.

'What's he saying?' Ezra asked.

'He says,' Sabine said and paused, as if having trouble translating. 'He says he knows what happened to your parents.'

A salvo from the TIEs' cannons hammered the *Ghost*, jostling everyone inside. Ezra broke free of Tseebo's grip, yet felt even more bound to the Rodian than before. Somewhere inside Tseebo's cybernetic implant was a truth that scared Ezra to his core.

'Sabine, I need you in the nose gun, now!' Hera yelled over the comm. Sabine, however, continued to stand in the doorway.

'Didn't you hear Hera?' Ezra said.

Sabine blinked. 'Didn't *you* hear Tseebo? He said he knows what happened to your parents!'

'I already know what happened,' Ezra said flatly. 'They're dead. So go.'

Sabine stared at Ezra, then left the room without another word. He grabbed Tseebo when she was gone. 'Are they,' Ezra said, swallowing, 'are my parents dead?'

A blast rattled Tseebo out of his silence. 'The troopers came. They took Mira and Ephraim Bridger away.'

'Where? Where did they take them?' Ezra demanded.

'Forgive Tseebo, forgive him.'

'Forgive you? For what?' Ezra asked.

'Tseebo failed. Tseebo was afraid. Tseebo could not raise Ezra Bridger.'

Ezra glared at the Rodian. His parents had trusted Tseebo, counted him as a close friend. 'Coward. You could've stopped them. Why didn't you stop them?'

'I ... I ...' Tseebo's eyes glazed over and he slipped back into his unresponsive state.

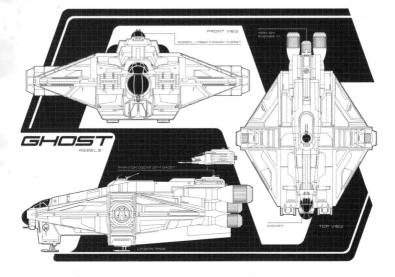

The *Ghost* shuddered as shots thudded against its hull. 'Shields down!' Hera's voice crackled on the comm. 'Ezra, I need you in the cockpit!'

Weeks earlier, Ezra wouldn't have listened. That wasn't true now. He wasn't like Tseebo. He wasn't a coward. He didn't hide when others needed him. Ezra helped his friends.

He hurried into the cockpit. Sparks danced across part of the console. 'Navicomputer's off-line!' Hera said. 'With Chopper down, you need to fix it.'

Ezra slid underneath the console. He hoped Chopper was repairable. The droid was a vital member of the crew and could've rerouted the damaged systems in a matter of microseconds. Ezra had rewired simple droid brains and jump bike engines, but nothing as sophisticated as a navicomputer. 'This isn't exactly my specialty.'

'Make it your specialty – and make it fast,' Hera said. 'Or this ship becomes a real ghost.'

Alarms went off. Out of the corner of his eye Ezra spotted triangular shapes appearing on a sensor scope. Imperial Star Destroyers. Two of them. Deploying more squadrons of TIEs.

Ezra began connecting wires as fast as he could. But without the tech manual, he doubted any of his repairs would make the navicomputer work.

'For fast travel over interstellar distances,

hyperspace is optimal,' Tseebo said.

Ezra poked his head up to find the Rodian standing in the cockpit. His implant blinked a pattern, then the console's hyperdrive status light came on. Tseebo had eliminated the need for the navicomputer by transmitting hyperspace coordinates directly to the ship.

'I don't believe it.' Hera reached for the lever. 'Hang on!'

The sensor scopes blanked as the *Ghost* jumped to lightspeed.

Admiral Kassius Konstantine strode down the bridge of the Star Destroyer *Relentless*. With him walked Baron Valen Rudor, Lothal's decorated TIE squadron commander. They conversed quietly, though said nothing about their present failure, since there was nothing to say. Losing the rebel freighter was one of the most embarrassing incidents in Konstantine's long and storied career.

He shouldn't receive all the blame. As

the Emperor's chief representative on the *Relentless*, the Inquisitor deserved some of it. The Inquisitor *had* been piloting one of the TIEs, after all. But Konstantine knew it would be unwise to remind the Inquisitor of that fact – particularly when the Inquisitor had been the only one to attach a tracking device on to the *Ghost*'s hull.

Konstantine and Rudor slowed as they approached the Inquisitor, who stood at the end of the bridge and stared out into space. 'We are receiving a signal from the tracker. They will not be able to outrun us for long,' Konstantine said.

The Inquisitor did not turn to acknowledge Konstantine. 'I still sense the Jedi and his Padawan within my grasp.'

Konstantine choked back a laugh. Jedi, Padawans – the Empire had wiped out their ancient religion years ago. Just because reports stated that the rebel leader wielded a lightsaber

didn't make him a Jedi.

The Inquisitor's blazing eyes locked onto Konstantine, full of malice and spite. Although the admiral had kept his opinion to himself, somehow the Inquisitor had guessed what he'd been thinking.

'We will catch them, sir,' Konstantine said, realising that if they didn't, his long and storied career might end rather suddenly.

CHAPTER **6**

As the *Ghost* sped along in hyperspace, the crew asked Ezra what should be done with Tseebo. Ezra said he didn't know and didn't care. The Rodian might have saved the *Ghost*, but he hadn't bothered saving Ezra's parents.

Tseebo, who had been staring blankly at a meiloorun fruit during the conversation, abruptly interjected that the *Ghost* was being tracked. It seemed impossible that this could happen while they were in hyperspace, but Tseebo said his implant had detected a new XX-23 tracer beacon on the ship's hull. A patched-up Chopper confirmed that fact, though he smugly reported that the tracker

was actually on the hull of the *Ghost*'s attached auxiliary craft, the *Phantom*.

Regardless, this new tracking technology meant that hyperspace was no longer an Imperial-free zone. For a vessel unlucky enough to carry one of these devices, the Empire could pinpoint exactly where it was travelling and send ships to meet the vessel at its destination.

Kanan, however, thought they could turn the tables against the Imperials. He suspected that the Inquisitor could sense his and Ezra's presence in the Force, so he devised a plan that used the two of them as bait. He and Ezra would detach the *Phantom* to lure the Imperials away from the *Ghost,* leaving the others free to transfer Tseebo into the safe custody of Fulcrum, the mysterious rebel leader.

Ezra didn't have a problem with being used as bait. It was to be expected if you were a member of the *Ghost* crew. His problem was the destination Kanan had picked.

Kanan piloted the *Phantom* over the pockmarked surface of asteroid PM-1203. 'You remember the nasty creatures Hera and Sabine found here?'

Ezra sure did. The crew had recently come to the asteroid's abandoned military outpost to pick up cargo from Fulcrum. Instead of meeting Hera's secretive contact, they'd had to fight off a pack of fanged beasts called fyrnocks. What Ezra had seen of the creatures gave him nightmares for a week.

'If we're going to survive this, you need to connect with them like I was trying to teach you before with the Loth-cat.' Kanan folded the *Phantom*'s wings and flew the ship inside the outpost's open hangar.

Ezra saw only darkness inside.

'Kanan,' he said, 'I'm afraid.'

Kanan landed the vessel. 'Got news for you, kid. Everyone's afraid. But admitting it makes you braver than most. It's a step forward.' He clasped Ezra's shoulder. 'I'll remove the tracking device. You make some new friends.'

Ezra followed Kanan out cautiously. As he walked to the front of the ship, he saw thin yellow slits staring back at him from the darkness. The fyrnocks were here – lots of them. For comfort Ezra whispered a mantra Kanan had taught him. 'One with the Force … one with the Force … I'm one with the Force.'

A couple of the creatures melted out of the

shadows. They pawed on all fours towards him, sniffing the air and arching their finned backs.

Ezra's legs turned to stumps. He couldn't move. The fyrnocks reared, spreading the skin flaps between limbs, ready to pounce.

Kanan stepped out of the darkness and pushed the fyrnocks back with the Force. 'Don't be afraid.'

'I'm not afraid of them.' Ezra had seen creepier cave dwellers at the Capital City zoo.

'Then what is it?' Kanan asked.

Ezra didn't know. Something else was scaring him. Something that had been building deep inside for years and just needed a trigger like the fyrnocks – like Empire Day – to erupt.

The creatures circled him. Kanan's hold on them was weakening. 'Ezra, what are you afraid of?' he shouted.

Ezra couldn't hold it in any longer. He had to let it out, the feelings of guilt, shame, and sadness that had pushed him away from

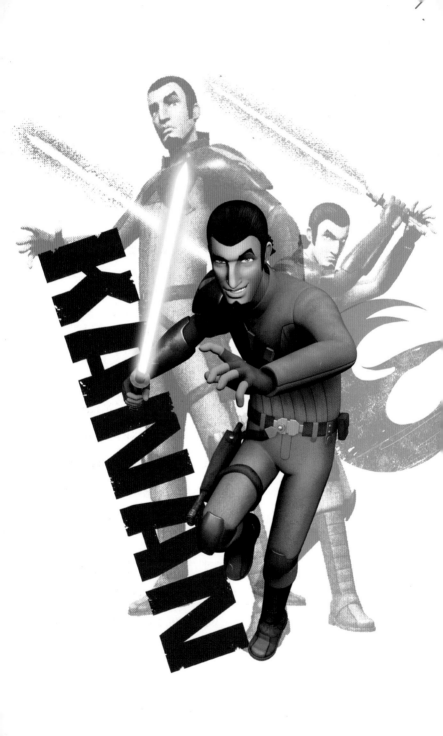

discovering what had happened to his parents.

'I'm afraid of knowing,' he confessed. 'I'm afraid of the truth.'

That was it, what troubled Ezra on this and every birthday. He feared that if he learned what had happened to his parents – what *truly* had happened – he might lose all hope. It had been easier to blame others than to admit his own fear.

'I'm sorry,' he said quietly. 'I forgive you, Tseebo.'

Just then Kanan lost his hold over the fyrnocks and they leapt at Ezra, all at once.

Ezra raised his hands, but didn't move. He didn't need to. The fyrnocks gave Ezra a friendly lick, then sat before him, as calm as house pets, connected through the Force.

In the common room of the *Ghost*, Tseebo stopped staring at the meiloorun fruit to look for Ezra Bridger. He had heard Ezra Bridger's apology, but oddly, Ezra Bridger wasn't in the room. His implant's sensors didn't even detect Ezra Bridger on the *Ghost*.

Perhaps the sensors were malfunctioning. Because if he could hear Ezra Bridger, Ezra Bridger should be able to hear him.

'I, too, am sorry,' Tseebo said. 'Forgive me, for everything.'

Relief flooded through Tseebo, a wave so strong and so raw that it overwhelmed his implant's emotional regulators. For the first time since his productivity enhancement, he put his hands on his spiny head and cried.

CHAPTER 7

The Inquisitor overruled

Admiral Konstantine's orders to deploy an entire battalion to asteroid PM-1203. Mere stormtroopers weren't going to catch these rebels. The troopers had failed many times before. The Inquisitor would go himself.

He stood in the cockpit of the shuttle and watched the descent towards an abandoned clone trooper base. The two presences inside couldn't hide themselves from him. One burned bright, like a torch; the other less so, but growing in intensity, like a candle that had just been lit.

The Jedi and his Padawan were in there. He could feel them.

The Inquisitor directed the shuttle pilot to land outside of the base's hangar, not wanting to alert the rebels unnecessarily. He then strode down the ramp with a contingent of the *Relentless*'s crack stormtroopers. The lead trooper, wearing a red shoulder pauldron, made a short-range scan. Such trivialities weren't necessary for the Inquisitor, but for the sake of the others, he let the man do his job. 'They're here all right. The rebel ship is inside,' the lead trooper said.

'Keep them contained,' the Inquisitor said. 'I want them alive.'

The lead trooper gathered some of the men, and they entered the hangar first, switching on the lights atop their blasters. The Inquisitor followed with the remainder of the landing party.

The rebel's puny attack shuttle lay inside. Next to the ship sat an adult human male

and a teenage boy, in a cross-legged posture with their eyes closed, the old Jedi fashion of meditation.

The Inquisitor smirked. This would be the last peace these two would ever have.

The troopers went to apprehend them, but

the Inquisitor hung back, alarmed. 'Wait. I sense –'

The troopers' glowlamps swept high. Perched above and behind the rebels were snarling, purple-skinned creatures with razorback fins and fangs like sharpened stalactites.

Eyes still closed, the Jedi adult and his boy apprentice both lifted their arms and indicated the Imperials.

The creatures roared and launched over the rebels, gliding on skin flaps that connected their limbs to their torsos. The stormtroopers' blaster fire was too late – the creatures had already sunk their teeth through their armoured uniforms.

The Inquisitor, however, stood firm, using the Force to hurl away every creature that came at him. He ignited his lightsaber and looked at the Jedi. 'This was your plan? To lure us here and allow these creatures to do your work for you?'

The Jedi opened his eyes and rose to face the Inquisitor. 'How do you think it's going?' He activated his blue blade.

One of the biggest beasts leapt at the Inquisitor. A wave of his hand was all that was required to send the creature flying backward. 'Pathetically.'

'Guess if you want something done right ...' the Jedi said, and attacked.

The Inquisitor parried the Jedi's swing, then went on the offensive himself. As in their last duel, the Jedi retreated. Try as he might, lunging and thrusting, he was no match for the Inquisitor's skill.

The Inquisitor sensed that the Jedi was trying to stall while his Padawan directed the creatures against the stormtroopers. Their plan would not work. The Inquisitor deflected another pitiful thrust, then vented his anger into the Force, tossing the human back into his ship. The impact echoed throughout the hangar and the Jedi dropped his lightsaber. Its blade

THE INQUISITOR

died as its wielder crumpled to the ground.

'Kanan!' The boy ran towards his master.

The Inquisitor grinned. *Kanan.* So that was the Jedi's name. 'Your meagre training is nothing in the face of true power,' he said to the boy, stepping towards the fallen Jedi.

The Jedi's lightsaber slid across the ground and flew into the boy's hand. The boy ignited the blade and held it high above his master. 'You're not going near him.'

The Inquisitor stared at the pathetic child. It was evident he had the talent and could be twisted into a useful tool. But he had *so much* to learn.

With a flick of his fingers, the Inquisitor yanked the lightsaber out of the boy's grip and summoned it to his free hand. 'I believe it's time to end both Jedi and Padawan, for good.'

Hera's secret contact, Fulcrum, arranged for the *Ghost* to dock with an Alderaanian blockade runner in deep space. To protect Fulcrum's identity, only Hera was allowed to transfer Tseebo to the ship.

As she led the Rodian towards the airlock, she noticed he moved like an ordinary being and had overcome his habit of staring blankly. But he also appeared troubled.

'Will Tseebo see Ezra Bridger again?' he asked.

'I hope so,' Hera said. 'Anything you'd like me to tell him?'

Tseebo looked away, not in his old distracted manner, but as if he were ashamed. 'Tseebo failed Bridgers. Did not watch over their son. But Tseebo try to make it right by accessing Imperial files on Ezra Bridger's parents. Tseebo knows Bridgers' fate.'

Hera stopped. What Tseebo knew might give Ezra closure to his troubles. She put her hand on Tseebo's shoulder. 'Tell me, Tseebo. Tell me and I'll tell Ezra.'

Tseebo nodded and told her.

Ezra pressed his heels into the floor when the Inquisitor tried to push him back with the Force. But like a Loth-rat in a grass storm, he couldn't hold. He tumbled backward, across the hangar, regaining his balance just in time to stop from plunging down a chasm-sized blast hole.

The Inquisitor advanced, wielding both blades. 'Your devotion to your master is admirable, but it will not save you. Nothing can.'

Ezra glanced at Kanan, who lay unmoving in a heap near the *Phantom*. Kanan had promised that if Ezra directed the fyrnocks to attack, he would take care of the Inquisitor. Yet once again, Kanan had lost his duel, leaving Ezra to deal with this villain all by himself.

'Good,' the Inquisitor said with a smile. 'Unleash your anger. I will teach you what your master couldn't.'

'You don't have anything to teach me,' Ezra snapped, though he began to question Kanan's recent lessons. Why had Kanan wasted time teaching him how to connect with nature, when what he really needed to learn was how to fight with the Force?

'The darkness is too strong for you, orphan. It is swallowing you up, even now,' the Inquisitor said.

'No.' Ezra wanted to punch the Inquisitor in the gut. Everything he said was a lie.

'Your master will die.'

'No!' Ezra repeated. The urge to do violence to the Inquisitor grew even stronger.

The Inquisitor refused to shut up. 'Your friends will die. And everything you've hoped for will be lost.'

Ezra couldn't listen any longer. He hated the Inquisitor. He hated him so much he wanted to make him feel pain, the same sadness and despair Ezra had felt over the years. He could feel those emotions churning inside of him, even behind him, becoming something large. Something strong. Something that the Inquisitor couldn't block. A force of pure rage.

A fyrnock.

Rising from the blast hole in the hangar floor, the creature cast a huge shadow over Ezra. Surprise flashed in the Inquisitor's eyes. This was no ordinary fyrnock. This was the mother of the fyrnocks. Ezra had connected with her to do his bidding.

'Ezra ... no!' he heard his master say. It must have been another of the Inquisitor's tricks. Kanan Jarrus was dead. And now it was time for the Inquisitor to die.

Ezra pointed at the enemy he hated and the shadow whipped over him like a cold current. The Inquisitor was knocked backward, losing hold of Kanan's lightsaber.

Ezra didn't see what happened next. He collapsed from exhaustion.

CHAPTER **8**

Kanan Jarrus wasn't dead, but his body felt as if he could've died. He struggled to his feet, aching from the Inquisitor's attack. Chaos ruled the hangar around him. The vicious fyrnocks were wreaking havoc with the stormtroopers while their mother was giving the Inquisitor the fight of his life.

Kanan stumbled over to Ezra. The boy was shivering. 'Kanan ... what happened? I feel so cold.'

Kanan held Ezra tightly for a moment, channelling some of his own warmth into the boy. 'It's OK. We're leaving.'

He grabbed his lightsaber and helped Ezra up and towards the *Phantom*. The Imperials were too busy with the fyrnocks to prevent them from boarding.

Kanan put Ezra in the rear, then took the pilot's chair. He neglected the warm-up procedures and just punched the engines into overdrive, triggering the guns at the same time.

Stormtroopers dove every which way to avoid being hit as the *Phantom* roared out of the hangar. Glancing down, Kanan glimpsed the Inquisitor exiting as well. The carcass of the mother fyrnock steamed behind him, but he did not look happy. Kanan had a feeling that his Emperor would not be happy, either.

Zooming over the Inquisitor's shuttle, Kanan strafed it with lasers, hitting some critical systems and stalling any possible pursuit. He then looped the *Phantom* around the asteroid to gain as much distance as he could from the Star Destroyers without eating up all the fuel reserves. When they were far

KANAN

enough away, he cut the engines to minimal velocity so the *Phantom* would be virtually undetectable until its mother ship, the *Ghost*, arrived.

'Something doesn't feel right,' Ezra said.

Kanan looked back. The boy's arms clung to his body, as if to hold himself together.

'When you open yourself to the Force,' Kanan said, 'if your will isn't strong enough, you are vulnerable to the dark side. Your good intentions can be twisted into something else if you feel fear or anger.'

'I was trying to protect you.'

'I know,' Kanan said. 'But your anger at the Inquisitor and your fear that I would die took you to the edge of the dark side. Your emotions caused the giant creature to attack.'

Ezra seemed puzzled. 'I don't remember it.'

Kanan sighed. 'That's for the best.' He'd known teaching was difficult – but he hadn't realised *how* difficult. 'It's my fault. I didn't teach you what you needed to know. I'm sorry.'

They spoke no more as they waited for the *Ghost*.

Ezra climbed down the ladder into the *Ghost*. He felt empty, weary, as if he hadn't slept for weeks, though technically, an entire standard day hadn't passed. It was still Empire Day. And it wasn't over yet.

The crew gave Ezra and Kanan a warm greeting in the common room. But Ezra didn't feel like celebrating. He walked out before Hera could talk to him.

'Ezra needs a little time to himself right now,' Kanan explained.

Ezra climbed into the nose turret and plopped down into the gunnery seat. This was where he'd had his first view of hyperspace. It hadn't been that long ago, yet it felt like ages. So much had changed in that short time. His world, his friends, *him*.

'Rough couple of days?' Sabine asked, entering the turret.

'Yeah. It's been ... weird.'

'Then I have just what you need.' Sabine took out a holodisk from her pouch. Dirty and scratched, it was the same holodisk that Ezra had ejected from his parents' secret console.

'It was pretty degraded. But I cleaned it up and found something.' She inserted the disk into the gunner's station and keyed the built-in projector. A two-dimensional hologram of a much younger Ezra and his parents shimmered in the air.

'Happy birthday, Ezra Bridger,' Sabine said.

Ezra stared at the parents he loved. His weariness gave way to a rush of joy. Soon he shared the same smile as his seven-year-old self.

This Empire Day would be a day long remembered.

PART 2
ENLIGHTENMENT

CHAPTER 9

Kanan knocked on the door to Zeb and Ezra's cabin, but the boy wasn't there, again. He'd already rescheduled this training session twice because Ezra had forgotten about it. But today's absence wasn't a slip of the mind. The kid wasn't taking his Jedi lessons seriously.

Kanan went into his cabin and removed the Holocron from his bunk's hidden drawer. The frustration he felt would be best channelled elsewhere. He sat cross-legged on the floor and began to meditate.

The more he relaxed, the less he felt of himself. In his mind's eye, he could see the Holocron hovering before him. Images appeared to him, of people and places he knew and didn't know. He heard voices, echoes of Jedi Masters of yore dispensing bits of wisdom.

To understand the Force, you must teach the Force...

Always be firm, but fair...

Never smile for your Padawan until they pass the trials, else an unruly apprentice you will have...

A creak in the corridor outside alerted him that someone was approaching. Kanan withdrew from the Force and lowered the Holocron to the ground.

The door opened. 'Sorry I'm late. Was with Sabine.' Ezra was breathing heavily, as if he had been running.

Kanan sighed, opening his eyes. 'Ezra, when we were on that asteroid, you made a dangerous connection through the Force. I have to know if you are ready.'

'I am ready,' Ezra insisted, then caught himself. 'Ready for what?'

'For a test, a real challenge. One that could determine if you are meant to be a Jedi,' Kanan said, 'or not.'

'But you said I was a Jedi. Why else would you be training me?'

Kanan took the Holocron and rose. 'I never said you were a Jedi. I said you have the potential to become one. But you lack discipline, focus.'

'C'mon,' Ezra retorted, 'you know how I grew up. I'm not used to all these rules.'

Kanan shook his head. 'You're lucky I'm not my master. She'd never let you get away with –'

'All the things you tried to get away with?' Ezra said.

Kanan looked at the door. 'You want a second chance or not? Go prep the *Phantom*.'

'As you say, Master,' Ezra said. For once, there was no sarcasm in the boy's voice.

Kanan bowed his head after Ezra left. Was he giving this kid too many chances because of his own failures as a teacher? What if

Ezra succumbed to the dark side because of something he didn't teach?

'You have to do this, Kanan.'

He looked up to see Hera standing in the doorway. 'After what happened on the asteroid, you have to help him,' she said.

'I hope I can,' Kanan said.

'I know you can.' She took his hand. Though she couldn't lend any support through the Force, she nonetheless cheered him in ways the Force never could.

A test. A real Jedi test. The thought excited Ezra. At last Kanan was going to teach him something worthwhile, instead of communing with Loth-cats or blocking rocks.

Nevertheless, his master refused to say where the two of them were flying. Kanan set the *Phantom* to autopilot, then headed to the back and sat down across from Ezra. Ezra knew he was in for a long lecture.

'When I was your age,' Kanan began,

'there were around ten thousand Jedi Knights defending the galaxy. We had small outposts, temples, spread throughout the stars.'

Ezra imagined what those last days of the Republic had been like. Would his life have been different? Would he have been schooled in one of those temples? What had happened to them?

'The Empire sought out these temples and destroyed many of them – but not all,' Kanan said. 'I want you to meditate, let the Force guide you to one of them.'

Ezra stared at his master. How could he find a lost Jedi temple when he couldn't even find yesterday's dirty socks?

'Trust yourself,' Kanan said. 'Trust the Force.'

Ezra nodded and closed his eyes. He would try, at least – though he knew Kanan's proverb: Do. Or do not. There is no try.

The problem was he didn't know what he was looking for. A pyramid? A cathedral?

KANAN

A monastery atop a cliff? And where? What solar system? How could they find a Jedi temple when the *Phantom* didn't even have a hyperdrive?

'Did you take this test at my age?' Ezra asked.

'Everything was different back then. All that remains now is the Force.'

The Force – *that* Ezra could feel. He felt it in the birds around their ship. He felt it in the blades of grass growing below. He even felt it in the occasional mound that interrupted the plains. One large stone stood out, like a strange artifact from another age. Stranger still was when the Force took Ezra's mind inside, as if solid rock was nothing. He found himself in a chamber that narrowed into a tunnel, where at its end blazed a bright, bright star.

Ezra opened his eyes. There was no need for a hyperdrive. The Jedi temple was right there, on Lothal.

He didn't know the coordinates, but his sense of it was so strong he directed Kanan to fly there. They landed in the middle of the plains, near a huge rock that resembled the one in Ezra's vision.

Kanan flipped a switch. 'Autopilot disengaged.'

Ezra looked at Kanan. If the autopilot was on the entire time, it meant –

'You already knew of this place,' he said, annoyed he'd done all that work for nothing.

Kanan landed the *Phantom*. 'I checked the Holocron back in my cabin. It holds extensive star maps, but I was as surprised as you that there was a temple here.'

They disembarked from the ship and approached the stone. Since Ezra had found the temple, Kanan said it was up to him to figure out a way inside.

'Seriously, can't you give me a hint?' Ezra asked.

'Don't look. Listen. Use the Force to hear the stone and its story.'

Ezra walked around the stone. It was solid, without anything resembling an entrance. When he closed his eyes and he lifted his hand, however, he began to feel the world around the stone. The temple was not in the rock, but under it.

'It wants to admit me,' Ezra said. '*Us*. Master and Padawan. Together.'

'Then together it shall be,' Kanan said.

Energy surged through Ezra's raised arm, pouring out towards the stone. He tensed under an immense strain, as if he was a small muscle working in tandem with a stronger one. The ground quaked and there was a tremendous cracking.

Ezra opened his eyes. 'Whoa.'

The huge stone had been corkscrewed partially out of the ground, revealing a hollow cavity buried beneath. He figured that must be the entrance to the Jedi temple.

'Don't lose focus. We don't want this thing crashing down on us,' Kanan said, lowering his arm.

Ezra descended into the hollow, glancing over his shoulder in astonishment. The stone must have weighed as much as a speeder bus, yet he had rooted it from the ground without ever touching it.

This kind of Jedi lesson made Ezra want to learn more.

CHAPTER **10**

Jedi temples reflected the personality of their architect, Kanan knew. The Jedi who had constructed this place must have had a fondness for the mysterious, for the large chamber Kanan and Ezra had entered led only into a tunnel of darkness. The chamber got darker still when the stone fell over the entrance, sealing them inside.

Kanan turned on a glowrod. 'You lost focus.'

'Dead guys are distracting,' Ezra said.

The glowrod revealed what Ezra was referring to. Bones of two former visitors lay strewn across the floor.

Kanan hoped the kid wouldn't be distracted

for the next part of the test, which would be much more challenging. 'In here, you'll have to face your worst fears and overcome them. And there's no guarantee of success.'

'I have plenty of faith,' Ezra said with a grin. 'Faith you'll keep me on track.'

'I'm not going with you,' Kanan said.

Ezra's grin became a grimace. 'Where are you going to be?'

'With them.' Kanan indicated the skeletons. 'Masters whose Padawans never returned.'

Ezra glanced at the bones, then at the darkness in the tunnel beyond. With a wary step, he walked towards it. 'What exactly am I looking for?'

'Nothing and everything,' Kanan said.

'That doesn't help,' Ezra said, his voice growing distant.

'I know,' Kanan said. The door to the tunnel shut and he knew Ezra could no longer hear him. 'But that's what my master told me.'

He wished Master Depa Billaba was still around to give him advice. She had been a Jedi Master of great wisdom and would know how best to teach Ezra.

Kanan sank into the Force to calm himself. Meditation, at least, gave him peace.

Even on his glowrod's brightest setting, Ezra could barely see a metre ahead of him. The tunnel's darkness was like a shroud, concealing everything. It wasn't until he had stepped into a junction that he realised the tunnel was splitting.

From there, many tunnels went off in different directions, none that he could see down. He started towards one tunnel, then moved towards another. Usually he had a hunch about what to do in situations like that. There he was in the dark. So he did what any normal kid would do. He recalled a rhyme his mother had taught him.

'Loth-rat, Loth-cat, Loth-wolf, run. Pick a

path and all is done –'

Before he moved his finger to the last tunnel, Kanan emerged from the darkness behind him. 'Really? That's how you're choosing? What happened to using the Force?'

'What happened to having faith in me?' Ezra asked.

'Second thoughts.' Kanan turned and marched down a side tunnel.

Ezra scowled. First the autopilot, now this. When would his master actually trust him?

Kanan walked fast, not waiting for Ezra. Ezra increased his pace, yet so did Kanan, disappearing around a corner. 'Kanan! Slow down!'

Then he heard the hiss of a lightsaber and a cry of pain.

Ezra sprinted around the corner. Kanan was on his knees, clasping a wounded arm, at the brink of a deep chasm. The Inquisitor stood over him, his red blade illuminating his yellow eyes. 'I felt a disturbance in the Force the moment the Jedi decided to bring you here, Padawan. Now, who dies first?'

Ezra stood petrified. The fear that iced his veins wasn't from some unresolved emotion. This was the pure, unbridled fear that he was going to die as the Inquisitor came towards him.

'No!' Kanan roared. He ignited his lightsaber and swung, blocking the Inquisitor's blade before it chopped Ezra in two. 'I'll die before I let you have the boy.'

The Inquisitor spun to strike back. Kanan parried the Inquisitor's relentless attack, but as in the other two duels, he was forced to give ground. Unlike those duels, however, this third one had a different outcome – a fatal one.

The Inquisitor slipped a quick thrust under Kanan's guard and into his chest. Kanan dropped his lightsaber and, with a whimper, fell into the chasm.

This time, Ezra knew Kanan was gone for

good. Not even a Jedi would be able to survive a fall like that.

'I'll make you pay. I swear you'll pay,' he snarled at the Inquisitor. Harnessing the same focus he'd used to levitate the stone, he called his master's lightsaber to his hand.

He was relieved when it came to him – and crushed when the hilt split apart into two pieces.

The Inquisitor laughed. 'Apparently someone's not quite ready to become a Jedi. And never will be.' He swung his lightsaber.

Ezra leapt away, avoiding the blade but not the chasm. He slipped and fell backward, spiralling down into what seemed to be a bottomless pit.

CHAPTER 11

The pit did have a bottom. A cold, metal one Ezra landed on so hard he felt his eyes bounce in their sockets. Yet despite the pain of the impact, somehow, he had survived.

He stood and looked around. The floor was metallic for a reason. He was in his bunk aboard the *Ghost*.

Zeb's voice boomed from elsewhere in the ship. 'How you figure the kid's doing?'

Ezra snuck across the corridor. Through an open doorway, he saw the crew lounging inside the common room.

Chopper answered Zeb's question with a dismissive beep. 'I have to agree with Chop,'

Hera said. 'I don't think we'll be hearing from Ezra again, which is too bad, because he had skills useful to our cause.'

'That's pretty cold, guys,' Sabine said, glancing at the doorway.

Ezra side-stepped against the corridor wall to remain unseen. But he was happy she'd defended him. Maybe in a few years, it'd work out between the two of them. Ezra and Sabine –

'After all he's just a little kid. Scared. Alone. I pity him.'

Her words had the impact of her detonation charges. Ezra shrank against the wall, his heart blown to bits.

'Well, look who's here!' Zeb reached through the door and yanked Ezra into the common room.

Chopper, Hera, and Sabine stared at Ezra as if he were an Imperial spy. Ezra turned away. He dried the tears from his eyes with his arm.

And that was when he knew this wasn't real.

His friends wouldn't say such things. They had risked their lives for him countless times, as he had for them. He – and they – were family.

'No, this isn't you talking,' Ezra said. 'I'm not back on the *Ghost*. I couldn't be.'

He heard a lightsaber igniting and knew

who held it before he turned. The Inquisitor had appeared behind the crew, ready to strike.

'No, no, this isn't real,' Ezra said.

The Inquisitor responded by stabbing Chopper. The droid shrilled a death rattle as his mechanical innards sparked.

Ezra ran towards his cabin. Behind him, his friends shrieked and cried for his help. He reminded himself that this wasn't real. If what they'd said before wasn't real, then their deaths weren't real either. This all must be an illusion.

He opened the door to his cabin and dove inside.

Ezra fell onto a stone floor. He looked up to see he was back in the outer chamber of the Jedi temple on Lothal.

The two skeletons lay untouched, but there was no Kanan. Had he really followed Ezra into the tunnel? Had his death been real?

Ezra couldn't reenter the tunnel to check. A door with no handle closed it off.

He pounded on the chamber wall. This test made no sense. Kanan had told him the Jedi were the guardians of peace and justice throughout the galaxy. Why would they create a test so difficult – so horrible – that it killed both master and apprentice?

Unless those skeletons were also illusions, designed to pressure the test-taker to face their ultimate fears.

Ezra turned towards the inner tunnel door. With a sudden whoosh, it slid up before him. He stepped back, startled. Had *he* somehow opened the door through the Force?

The Inquisitor spoiled that hope. 'How perceptive,' he said, striding out of the darkness.

No. This was impossible. This couldn't be the Inquisitor. Not the real one. 'You were on the *Ghost*. And that – all that – was definitely an illusion,' Ezra said.

'It may have been. But I assure you, *I* am not.' The red blade that sizzled out of the

Inquisitor's hilt seemed to confirm that. Ezra backed away, bumping into the chamber wall.

'No way out,' the Inquisitor said.

'There's always a way out, if I follow my training.' Ezra scrunched his brow, trying to focus – trying to convince himself that none of this was real.

'Are you afraid to face your demise?' the Inquisitor said, coming closer.

'No. Afraid of being alone again? Sure. Afraid of letting down my master? Absolutely.'

The Inquisitor chuckled. 'Your 'master' lies dead and rotting in a forgotten tunnel. You could hardly have let him down more.'

Ezra couldn't take those words to heart. Because he knew Kanan had believed in him. Kanan had sacrificed his own life so that Ezra could escape. Ezra would be disgracing Kanan's memory if he believed the Inquisitor's lies.

'I'm not afraid,' he said.

The Inquisitor snarled and swung. Ezra closed his eyes. He didn't feel the blade slice into him. He felt nothing at all.

'Big fears have you faced, young one,' said a voice that sounded like a mischievous old-timer with an amphibian in his throat. 'Come, see more clearly what you could not see before.'

Ezra opened his eyes. He had all his limbs and wasn't wounded. Best of all, the Inquisitor was gone. In his place floated a point of light that reminded Ezra of the will-o'-the-wisps travelers had reported in Lothal's marshes. 'Who are you?' he asked.

'A guide,' the voice said.

The light moved into the tunnel. Ezra pocketed his glowrod and followed.

Kanan couldn't meditate. His mind kept racing. He was worried about the kid. Might this have been a mistake? Might Ezra be too old for this test? When Kanan was trained, Jedi younglings were schooled at a very early age, so that fears from the outside world couldn't corrupt them.

Kanan opened his eyes. The temple's outer chamber was as it had been, empty of everything but the two skeletons. The door to the tunnel remained closed. Ezra must still be in the inner temple. What was taking the kid so long?

'Patience,' said a familiar voice. 'Remember you nothing of your own training?'

'Master Yoda?' Kanan peered around the empty chamber. 'I must be losing it.'

'Lost, yes. But what lost, hmmm? The question, that is,' the voice answered.

It *was* Master Yoda. No other Jedi talked like that.

Kanan dropped to his knees. 'Master, how can this be?'

'Be not concerned with *how*. Know I am here, because *you* are here. Changed something has.'

Kanan mustered a false bravado as he spoke. 'I have taken on an apprentice.'

'Apprentice? And now *master* are you?'

Kanan bowed his head. Master Yoda was right to reprimand him. He'd been imprudent to believe he could teach a Padawan, when his own training had been cut short when he was Ezra's age.

'I'm not sure of my decision,' Kanan said. 'Not because of him or his abilities, but because of me, because of who I am.'

'And who is that?'

Kanan knelt in silence. Hera had asked him that same question in different ways. It was the one question he feared answering.

'I've lost my way for a long time, but now I have a chance to change things.' He looked at the door to the inner temple. 'I won't let Ezra lose his way, not like *I* did.'

Their exchange brought Kanan to a realisation. This test was not designed solely for the apprentice. It was also a test for the master, for facing one's fears was a lifelong struggle.

CHAPTER 12

The point of light brought Ezra to a junction of three tunnels. But its voice refused to tell him which one to travel down.

'Your path you must decide.'

Ezra considered the tunnels, right, left, then centre, sensing nothing in the Force. Picking one seemed arbitrary. But maybe that was the point. It didn't matter which tunnel he chose, as long as he remained committed to his choice. Just like he should be committed to his training.

He headed down the centre tunnel because it gave him a sense of balance. The path of the Jedi did not twist and turn – it was clear

and consistent, with no shortcuts for its challenges.

Ezra entered a cavern so massive it had its own night sky, sparkling with constellations he didn't recognise. One resembled a round face with long, pointy ears.

'Tell me,' the voice said. 'Why must you become a Jedi?'

Ezra gazed at the stars. 'Well, I'll become stronger, powerful – and I'd make the Empire suffer for everything it did. For everything it took. For my parents.'

'Jedi way is revenge?' the voice inquired. 'Teach you this, your master did?'

'No,' Ezra said. 'Kanan's a good master, a great master.' The stars started to revolve in the sky and the cavern floor disappeared, except for a silver ring around Ezra's feet.

'Then why seek you revenge?'

'I don't,' Ezra insisted.

'Inside you, much anger. Much fear.'

The voice was right. But Ezra had other qualities, positive ones he'd only recently discovered. 'Before I met Kanan, I only ever thought of myself,' he conceded. 'But Kanan and the others don't think like that. They help people, they give everything away. I see it, I see how it makes people feel.'

'Feel, yes, how?' asked the voice.

'Alive.' Ezra recalled his first trip to Tarkintown, when Zeb and Sabine handed out food and lifted the spirits of the starving refugees. 'They feel alive. Like I do now.'

Ezra was awash in stars. The constellations spun above him, around him, and even beneath the silver disc on which he stood. Then one point of light descended from the rest.

'Ahead of you a difficult path there is,' said the voice. 'A Jedi you may yet be.'

Ezra stretched out his hand. The light landed, in the form of a crystal.

When the door to the inner tunnel slid open and Ezra walked out, Kanan couldn't mask his relief. 'How are you?'

'Different, but the same,' Ezra said.

'I know what you mean.' And Kanan did. While Master Yoda had helped him accept that he was the right teacher to train Ezra, he still had doubts as to how best to instruct the boy. But that was natural. He wouldn't be a good teacher if he didn't question his own methods.

'I found this.' Ezra opened his hand. A small, shiny crystal rested on his palm. 'It's good, right?'

'That's a kyber crystal.' Kanan had never seen one so beautiful.

'Oh ... wow!' Ezra stared at the crystal, then looked at Kanan. 'What's that?'

Kanan rewarded his pupil with a sly grin. After he told Ezra what the Jedi used the crystals for, the kid couldn't have been more excited if he'd won ten million credits.

The effort to levitate the boulder was child's play next to the concentration required to tune the kyber crystal. But once Ezra got back onto the *Ghost*, he maintained his level of focus. He spent days and nights in his cabin, tinkering with the spare parts the crew had given him. Every component had to work in perfect order with the crystal, else the whole device would be scrap.

When he had finished, he went into the *Ghost*'s common room, where his friends waited. He gave the object that he'd constructed to Kanan for approval.

'Well, it's different. But that seems right for you.' Kanan returned the cylindrical object to Ezra. 'Go for it.'

Ezra took a breath, then pressed the activation button. A bright blue blade sprang to life and hummed as Ezra swung it gently through the air.

Kanan, Hera, Zeb, Sabine, and even Chopper, with his dome lights, glowed with pride. Ezra had aced Kanan's lesson. He had made his connection to the crystal.

He had built his own lightsaber.

ABOUT THE AUTHOR

MICHAEL KOGGE has written in the *Star Wars* galaxy for a long, long time. He penned the junior novelisation for *Star Wars Rebels – The Rebellion Begins*, along with many other books in the Rebels series. His graphic novel *Empire of the Wolf*, an epic tale of werewolves in ancient Rome, was recently published by Alterna Comics. He lives in Los Angeles, residing online at www.michaelkogge.com.